Dear mouse friends,
Welcome to the world of

Geronimo Stilton

THE RODENT'S GAZETTE
EDITORIAL STAFF

Geronimo Stilton
A learned and brainy
mouse; editor of
The Rodent's Gazette

Thea Stilton
Geronimo's sister and
special correspondent at
The Rodent's Gazette

Trap Stilton
An awful joker;
Geronimo's cousin and
owner of the store
Cheap Junk for Less

Benjamin Stilton
A sweet and loving
nine-year-old mouse;
Geronimo's favorite
nephew

Geronimo Stilton

THE HAUNTED CASTLE

Scholastic Inc.

New York   Toronto   London   Auckland
Sydney   Mexico City   New Delhi   Hong Kong

ISBN 978-0-545-10374-9

Based on an idea by Elisabetta Dami.
www.geronimostilton.com

Published by Scholastic Inc., 557 Broadway, New York, NY 10012.
SCHOLASTIC and associated logos are trademarks and/or registered trademarks of Scholastic Inc.

Stilton is the name of a famous English cheese. It is a registered trademark of the Stilton Cheese Makers' Association. For more information, go to www.stiltoncheese.com.

Text by Geronimo Stilton
Original title *Ritorno a Rocca Taccagna*
Cover and interior illustrations by Claudio Cernuschi (pencils and ink) and Valentina Grassini (color)
Graphics by Merenguita Gingermouse, Sara Baruffaldi, and Yuko Egusa

Special thanks to Beth Dunfey
Translated by Julia Heim
Interior design by Kay Petronio

12 11 10 9 8 7 6 5 4 3 2   11 12 13 14 15 16/0

Printed in the U.S.A.   40
First printing, July 2011

PHONE CALL FOR MR. STILTON!

It began like any other ordinary morning.

As usual, I woke up in a great mood.

As usual, I scurried over to my office.

As usual, I squeaked "good morning" to all my colleagues.

Oh, excuse me. I almost forgot to introduce myself. My name is Stilton, *Geronimo Stilton*. I am the editor of the most famouse

newspaper in New Mouse City, *The Rodent's Gazette.*

The staff began our daily editorial meeting. We were in search of an IDEA for a new column. But none of us could agree on what it should be **ABOUT**.

As the reporters were pitching a few concepts, the phone rang.

Ring, ring, rinnnnnnng!

I picked up the receiver. "Hello, Stilton here, *Geronimo Stilton*!"

Bzzzzz . . . bzzzzzzzzzzzz . . .

It was a **bad connection**.

An operator with a nasal squeak cut in. "Mr. Stilton, will you accept a **collect call**?"

Bzzz . . . bzzzzzz . . .

The line kept buzzing.

Who could be calling me

collect? It was so **strange**!

"A **collect call** means **YOU PAY** for the phone call!" the operator explained. Well, of course I knew that! "Do you accept the charges? Hmmm? Do you accept or not? I need an answer here! I don't have all day to twiddle my whiskers while you make up your mind, you know!"

"Oh, I'm sorry. I was a bit distracted by the buzzing on the line," I explained. "I accept, of course!"

Suddenly, I heard a **familiar** voice squawk, "Geronimo? Is that you, Geronimo?"

Bzzzzzz . . . bzzz . . .

I **recognized** that squeak right away. It belonged to my **Uncle Samuel S. Stingysnout**!

My Whiskers Were Shaking . . .

"Geronimo!" Uncle Samuel shouted. "I'm calling to invite you to 𝔭enny 𝔭incher ℭastle for the **ceremony** that will take place on October thirty-first. Will you come or not?"

I didn't have a clue what he was talking about. "What **ceremony**?" I asked.

"You know, the **ceremony**, Geronimo!" he yelled. "**THE C-E-R-E-M-O-N-Y!**"

"Yes, I heard you, but what **ceremony** are you squeaking about?" I asked, trying to be polite.

"**GERONIMO!**" he hollered. "**ALL** the relatives are coming! The only one who won't be there is **YOU**!"

I was starting to lose my patience. "But

what is this **ceremony**?"

He continued as though I hadn't spoken. "Plus I've organized everything! You wouldn't want me to **waste** all that effort, would you?" Before I could get a squeak in edgewise, he went on, "So it's all settled, then. I will expect you, Benjamin, THEA, and Trap for the **ceremony**. . . ."

At that point, my whiskers were shaking with exasperation. **"WHAT CEREMONY???"** I shrieked.

That was when we got cut off.

It was all so **strange**! You see, the relationship between the *Stilton* family and the **Stingysnout** family is strained, for one simple reason: The Stingysnouts are a bit **stingy**.

If you look up the word *stingy* in the DICTIONARY, you'll find this definition:

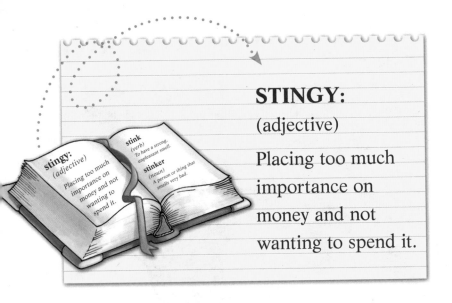

STINGY:

(adjective)

Placing too much importance on money and not wanting to spend it.

I told my sister THEA, my cousin Trap, and my nephew Benjamin that we had been invited to Penny Pincher Castle. These were their reactions:

"I don't want to go to Penny Pincher Castle! It's colder than iced cheese there — all because Uncle Samuel won't spend the money to turn on the heat."

"I don't want to go to Penny Pincher Castle! there's never anything to eat there — all because Uncle Samuel won't spend the money to put cheese in the fridge."

"I don't want to go to Penny Pincher Castle! It's so dark and spooky there — all because Uncle Samuel won't spend the money to turn on the lights."

The Stingysnout Family

The Stingysnouts come from the Valley of Lack, where the ancestral family home, Penny Pincher Castle, is located on top of Cheap Change Hill. For years, Uncle Samuel has lived there with his son, Stevie, and his younger sister, Chintzina.

Years and years ago, Samuel's great-grandfather, Cheddar Cheapskate Stingysnout, married Serena Stilton, Geronimo's great-grandmother. Despite being distantly related, the two families do not get along — mostly because the Stingysnouts are so cheap! The Stiltons and the Stingysnouts see each other only during family ceremonies, like weddings and funerals.

Samuel Stingysnout

The head of the Stingysnout family, Samuel, is a real master of frugality. His motto is "I need to set an example for the other Stingysnouts!" He prides himself on finding new (and often extreme) ways to save money. He's been known to wake before dawn so he can sneak over to his neighbor's house to read his newspaper instead of buying his own.

Samuel washes himself without soap so he doesn't have to purchase any. He refuses to spend money on toilet paper, and some family members believe he's been wearing the same pair of underwear for more than a decade. He even wears pants inside out so he doesn't have to wash them!

When Samuel makes tea, he dips the tea bag in the water for a second — PLUNK — and then he takes it out right away. "This way tea bags can last for years and years," he tells anyone who will listen. But perhaps his cheapest (and grossest) habit is this: After he brushes his fur, he pulls stray whiskers out of the comb and uses them as dental floss. Eww!

The Stingysnout Family

The Stingysnouts are distantly related to the Stiltons. Not all of them are able to make it to the ceremony (probably because they don't want to spend money on the trip!)

STEVIE Samuel's son. When it's time to bathe, he soaps himself up while he's still dry and turns on the shower at the last minute to save money on hot water.

CHINTZINA Samuel's younger sister. When she was a mouseling, she never laughed, because she didn't want to waste energy.

THRIFTELLA Stevie's cousin. For perfume, she uses only free samples.

SAMUEL S. STINGYSNOUT Geronimo's uncle. He wakes up early to read his neighbor's newspaper.

PENNIFORD AND SAVEANNA Ivy's children, Samuel's niece and nephew. They make cheddar pops last for three years by taking one lick at a time and then wrapping them up again.

WORTHINGTON Thriftella's twin brother. He always wears the same shirt; his secret is that he changes its patches every three years.

ALL RIGHT, I'LL GO

I convinced Thea, Trap, and Benjamin to **GO** anyway. After all, family is family! Plus it seemed like this ceremony was important.

"All right, I'll go." Thea sighed. "As long as we take my **convertible**. But Gerry Berry, what's the scoop on this **ceremony**?"

"All right, I'll go," Trap mumbled. "But no way am I getting in that girly **PINK** convertible. Let's go in my **van**.

My van is better!

My convertible is perfect!

And, Germeister, what's the deal with this **ceremony**?"

"All right, I'll go," Benjamin squeaked. "But can we please take an **airplane**? And, Uncle Geronimo, can you explain what this **ceremony** is?"

"All right, I'll go." I sighed. "Even though I don't have a clue what the **ceremony** is. But only if you all quit arguing! You know I can't stand **bickering**!"

Thea took advantage of the confusion and **JUMPED** into her car. "You're right,

All right, I'll go. . . .

A plane is the best!

The Road to Penny Pincher Castle

1. LONELINESS PASSAGE
2. PARSIMONIOUS PEAK
3. REDUCTION RIVER
4. THE VALLEY OF LACK
5. LITTLE LAKE
6. SCANTYTOWN
7. PENNY PINCHER CASTLE

Gerry. Let's stop this silly squabbling. Come on, everyone, hop in!"

Trap grabbed the map of Mouse Island. Once I managed to convince him he was holding it upside down, we figured out the **route** we needed to take. Thea revved up the engine, I clutched my stomach nervously (I always get carsick when she drives!), and we departed.

By **LATE EVENING**, we arrived at the Valley of Lack. It is called the Valley of Lack because it is **lacking** in everything. There is little water and very little light, so there are very *few* plants. There are even *fewer* animals: very *few* birds in the sky, very *few* fish in the rivers, and very *few* squirrels in the forest. Even the **inHaBitants** of the valley are *scarce,* and they squeak very *little* (to save their breath!).

To enter the valley, you must **cross** a *little*-known gorge called Loneliness Passage. Next you must bump along a very *infrequently* used **street**. (To save money, it has never been paved!)

At the end of the valley is the Reduction River, which merges with the river in New Mouse City. The river **water** is **ALWAYS** very *low*. At the end of the river is Little Lake, which holds just a drop of water, with *few* fish, *few* ducks, and *few* REEDS.

Before arriving at Penny Pincher Castle, you must pass through a small city called Scantytown, which can be reached by only *one* road that has just *one* lane. In the village, we passed very *few* stores, only *one* town square, and very, very *few* rodents.

As we drove, the weather grew worse. The sky turned black and threatened to storm.

A freezing wind whipped up. Then it began to pour.

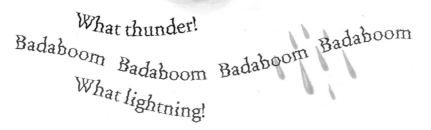

What thunder!
Badaboom Badaboom Badaboom Badaboom
What lightning!

Even my sister the speed rat was forced to drive slowly and carefully. We continued to the highest peak of the mountain, where **Penny Pincher Castle** was located.

As we drove, we saw a *lightning bolt* hit Uncle Samuel's castle!

Eeeeek! Benjamin leaped into my lap in terror. I leaped into Trap's.

WHAT A FRIGHT!

THE VERY SADDEST OF CEREMONIES

We knocked on the great door of **Penny Pincher Castle**. A thin rodent with hazel fur and **bushy** white eyebrows came out. He was dressed all in black, like an UNDERTAKER. It was **Uncle Samuel**!

He was crying so hard, tears were dripping down his snout like a fountain. He reached out and dried his **tears** on my **SLEEVE**!

"Hello, my dear niece and nephews, my most delicate cheese niblets," Uncle Samuel bawled. "Thank goodness you've arrived in time for the **ceremony**!"

"Certainly, certainly," I replied. "Um, Uncle Samuel . . . what exactly is this ceremony all about?"

Uncle Samuel **wiped** his tears on the collar of my **JACKET**.

"Aaaaaaaaaaaaaaaaaaaaaaaaaaaaaaaaaaaah, it's so sad . . . the very saddest of ceremonies!"

"Yes, so I see, but what kind of **ceremony** is it?" I asked.

Uncle Samuel dried more tears on my **JACKET** pocket. "Uuuuuuuuuuuuuuuuuhhhhh, I can't explain it. I'll just end up crying harder!"

"I understand. But could you at least tell us what the ceremony is called?" I asked desperately.

Uncle Samuel blew his snout on my **tie**. "Oooooooooooooooooooooooohhhhhhh,

THE VERY SADDEST OF CEREMONIES

all right, I will explain it. Brrrrgggghhh," he said, blowing his snout one last, long time.

I couldn't take it anymore. My jacket was drenched with his tears and my tie was green with his snot! "What **ceremony** is it? Just tell us!"

"Uuuuuuuuuuuuuuuuuuuuuuuuuuuuuuuuuuuh, since you insist, I will tell you: Uncle Bigwig Stingysnout has left us! That is, he's missing. . . . I mean, he's disappeared. . . . Well, I mean, he **passed away**!"

"Whaaaaat?" Thea, Trap, Benjamin, and I shouted.

"*Uncle Bigwig* passed away?" I asked. This was **strange**! I had no idea who Uncle Bigwig was. I looked at Thea, Trap, and Benjamin. They shrugged. **None** of us knew him!

At that moment, a lightning bolt struck a

few feet from us, illuminating the castle with a very **SINISTER** light.

"Eeeeeeeeek! This weather is downright terrifying!" I squeaked.

Uncle Samuel, on the other paw, was pleased. "I absolutely adore this weather! You see, when lightning strikes, there is no need to turn on the lights, and we can save money on our electric bill!"

"Uncle Samuel, can you please let us in?" Thea asked impatiently. "It's raining cats and rats out here!"

Uncle Samuel just giggled. "Splendid! There will be no need to take a shower, and we can save money on our water bill!"

I rolled my eyes. There was no reasoning with this rodent.

BUT JUST WHO WAS UNCLE BIGWIG?

Uncle Samuel let us in and *guided* us down a **dark hallway**, which had no electricity (to save money!). To *light* the way, he held up a five-armed candelabra with just **ONE** candle in it (to save money, of course!).

The castle seemed much more **run-down** than the last time I'd seen it.

It really was in need of some **RESTORATION**! Drops of **water** were falling from the ceiling, the floors were full of **HOLES**, and the walls were **moldy**.

"So, Uncle Samuel," Thea began, "just how old was *Uncle Bigwig*?"

Uncle Samuel murmured, "Um . . . maybe sixty . . . or seventy . . . no, he was eighty!"

"What kind of work did *Uncle Bigwig* do?" Trap asked.

"Uhm . . . maybe a **painter** . . . or a lifeguard . . . no, no, he was a lawyer!"

"Where did *Uncle Bigwig* live?" Benjamin inquired.

"Um . . . maybe in Mousefort Beach . . . or San Mouscisco . . . no, no, he lived in Scantytown!"

"So who exactly was *Uncle Bigwig*?" I demanded.

"Oh, Uncle Bigwig was the heir to **ALL THE** Stingysnout property!" Uncle Samuel said quickly. "It was all his! Even this castle belonged to him!"

I found this all very **strange**! How could this castle belong to a mouse none of us had ever heard of?

THE STILTON FAMILY

Finally, we arrived in the enormouse banquet hall. All the relatives were gathered there — the *Stiltons* and the **Stingysnouts**. First we saw Aunt *Sugarfur* and Uncle *Kindpaws* with the twins, **Squeakette** and *Squeaky*. Grandma **Rose** was there, too. She had left Grandpa **Hayfur** to care for the farm so that she could take part in the **ceremony** (which showed how important this **ceremony** was!).

In the middle of the room, standing tall, was *Grandpa William Shortpaws*. As soon as he saw me, he squeaked, "Well, well, well, Grandson. You're late as usual! Come on, move those paws!"

Next to Grandfather William were *Tina Spicytail*, Aunt *Sweetfur*, and Uncle *Grayfur*.

And of course Uncle Gagrat and Uncle Worrywhiskers never missed a big family event.

Suddenly, someone **BLASTED** a toy trumpet in my ear. I almost jumped out of my fur. "**AAAAAAGGGGHHHHH!**"

Once my ears stopped ringing, I shouted, "**WHO DID THAT**?"

Naturally, it was Uncle Gagrat, who is famouse for being the family prankster! "Got ya again, Geronimo!" he said triumphantly.

Trap giggled. "Good one! Germeister is such a 'fraidy mouse!"

I turned **RED** with EMBARRASSMENT. As you've probably guessed, Trap and Uncle Gagrat come from the same branch of the family tree.

The Stilton Family

UNCLE BIGWIG'S LAST WILL & TESTAMENT

Uncle Samuel announced, "It is time for Larry Legalmouse, Uncle Bigwig's lawyer, to read the *will*."

Larry Legalmouse entered. He was a skinny mouse who wore tiny spectacles on the tip of his snout. He consulted a **pile** of papers, cleared his throat, and *began*.

Blah blah blah...

"Ahem, well, here we are, right, rather, I mean, as it stands, considering, let me clarify, so that, despite the fact, **be that as it may**, surely, **but**, however . . ."

A rumble of impatience rose from the *Stilton* and **Stingysnout** families. Finally, Trap **shouted**, "Enough of this legal mumbo jumbo! Just cut to the cheese already!"

"Now, now, I know you're all **anxious** to hear what's in the will, but there's no need to be rude!" the lawyer declared. "**Just one minute!**" Then he cleared his throat and began to read the *will*:

"**I, Bigwig Stingysnout, leave all that I own to . . .**"

The whole family whispered, "To . . . ?"

"**I, Bigwig Stingysnout, leave all that I own to . . .**"

The whole family **shouted**: "To whoooooooommmm?"

"I, Bigwig Stingysnout, heir of the Stingysnout estate, leave all that I own, by which I mean Penny Pincher Castle, to Uncle Samuel and Uncle Samuel alone!"

"YES!" Uncle Samuel exclaimed. "Uncle Bigwig left me the **CASTLE**!" He pumped his paw in the air like a mouseling at a mouseketball game.

I, Bigwig Stingysnout, heir of the Stingysnout estate, leave all that I own, by which I mean Penny Pincher Castle, to Uncle Samael and Uncle Samuel alone!

Sincerely,
Bigwig Stingysnout

I found this all quite **STRANGE**!

Uncle Samuel cleared his throat. "In order to celebrate my new ownership of the **CASTLE**, I want to offer a drink to everyone: **A NiCE GLASS OF WATER**, which will refresh you (and help save money)."

I sighed. So did the rest of the family.

Then Uncle Samuel ANNOUNCED, "Then I will give a short — I mean very, very, very short — in fact, the very shortest of eulogies in honor of our dear Uncle Bigwig!"

With that, he **began** a long, very long, in fact, one might say it was the looooooooooooooooooooooooooooooongest of speeches.

"I will be brief, no, very brief, no, the briefest, I will not make a long speech — no, no, no, what I mean to say is that I don't want to bore you with my words, I will not keep you all here when you no doubt have better things to do, no, I will not speak for hours and hours, telling you all sorts of things that you don't care about, things that might be boring, things that might interest only me, what I mean is, things that are from my point of view, things I feel, things I notice, things I perceive, things you would avoid hearing if you could, well, what I am trying to say is that today I will not make a boring, rather very boring, in fact the most boring of funeral speeches, I imagine that if I did, you might fall asleep, ha, ha, ha, I realize that maybe you don't want to hear me, so I will be brief, no, I will be very brief, you will see how quickly my speech will end, I will be as quick as a gerbil on a wheel, I will only say a few, no, very, very few, no the fewest of words, only important things, what is essential, things that are basic, so I will repeat (as I have already said, I said it already, didn't I? I think I did, I think I told you already, of course, so, as I have already said . . .) so I repeat that I will be very brief, because I know long speeches are boring and I don't want to bore you, no, no, no, absolutely not, there is no way that I plan to bore my dear relatives, family is the most important thing in the world, ha, ha, ha, even though we are talking about death, your happiness is very important to me, so I will make a short and painless speech, I will try to sum up in a few, rather very few, that is, the fewest of words, the basic concepts, as it were. So as I was saying, it is time to bury Uncle Bigwig!"

VERY STRANGE INDEED!

Even though the **speech** was incredibly long and boring, I managed to stay awake. And I noticed that Uncle Samuel didn't say *anything* specific about Uncle Bigwig.

I found that quite **strange**!

As I chatted with the other Stilton and Stingysnout relatives, I noticed that not one of them seemed to know Uncle Bigwig. As far as I could tell, the only one who knew him was Uncle Samuel.

I found that very strange!

Out of curiosity, I went to look in the Stingysnouts' family album, which listed all the relatives — including their first names, last names, and PHOTOGRAPHS. But

the album was missing!

Who had taken it?

Who?

Who??

Who???

I found it all very, very strange!

Uncle Samuel moaned, "Ooohhh, poor, dear Uncle Bigwig! How he will be missed!" He accompanied us to a room next to the banquet hall. A **COFFIN** sat in the center of the room. Then he left, closing the door behind him.

Although I didn't remember Uncle Bigwig, I was still **SAD** that he was gone. So I headed toward the **COFFIN** to pay my respects.

Now, as you know, dear reader, I am not the most coordinated of rodents. Without meaning to, I tripped and bumped into the coffin. That was how I discovered it was so light it almost seemed . . . **empty!**

I extended my **paw** to see why it was so light ①, but right at that moment, **Uncle Samuel** returned and **yelled**, "Geronimo, stop, what are you doing? **Don't touch that!**" ② He was so alarmed he tripped, too! He bumped into the coffin and accidentally pushed it off the table — onto my paws! ③

"OOOUUUUCCHHH!" I shrieked. (4) But before I could move . . .

"No one touch the coffin!" Uncle Samuel commanded. "Uncle Bigwig . . . ummm . . . has left us because of a very contagious disease . . . er, acute ratitis!"

I was truly shocked. I had never, ever heard of acute ratitis!

I found that very strange indeed!

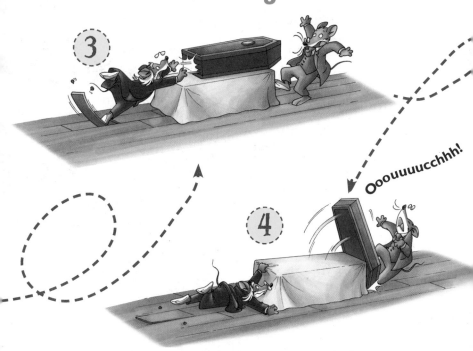

Ooouuuucchhh!

SWEET DREAMS!

By this time, it was quite **late** at night, and it was pouring rain outside.

"It's too late for a burial now," Thea declared.

"Quite right, my little **CHEESE PUFF**," said Grandfather William. Thea was his favorite grandchild. "We will bury Uncle Bigwig **TOMORROW**!"

Uncle Samuel reluctantly agreed. (He'd probably figured out a way to save **money** by burying Uncle Bigwig in the middle of the night!) He led us up a creaky staircase to our rooms. He was holding his usual five-armed silver candelabra with only one lit candle, because there was no electricity in the castle.

As we climbed, I couldn't help noticing that the candle's flame cast gloomy shadows on the walls. I heard Uncle Samuel whisper under his breath, "I can't bear to think of how much money this candle is costing me!"

PENNY PINCHER CASTLE

SOUTH SIDE

1. ENTRANCE
2. SITTING ROOM
3. KITCHEN
4. BEDROOM
5. BANQUET HALL
6. GREAT HALL
7. UNCLE SAMUEL'S STUDY
8. BATHROOM
9. LIVING ROOM
10. HALLWAY
11. BEDROOM
12. TREASURE ROOM

PENNY PINCHER CASTLE

NORTH SIDE
1. WELL
2. PANTRY
3–7. BEDROOMS

8–9. BATHROOMS
10. AUNT CHINTZINA'S
    STUDY
11. ATTIC

Uncle Samuel accompanied Thea, Trap, and Benjamin to their rooms. Then he led me a bit farther to a **DARK DOOR**, murmuring, "For you, *dear* nephew, I have saved the *best* room . . . the room where our *dearly departed* used to sleep. That's right — it's Uncle Bigwig's old room!" THEN HE BLEW HIS SNOUT ON MY tie.

I muttered, "Er, thank you, Uncle Samuel, but I can sleep somewhere else —"

"No, no, no, **I insist**. You will sleep here!" He opened the door, and the room **lit up** (well, barely, since we only had one candle). The walls were covered with peeling paint. In the middle of the room was a very, very old bed that wobbled on just three legs.

Uncle Samuel **BLEW HIS SNOUT ON THE SLEEVE OF MY JACKET**.

"Poor Uncle Bigwig . . . Everything is just the way he left it before he . . . well, you know . . . before he croaked!"

With that he left, muttering, "Good night, dear Nephew. A bit of advice: *Don't* think too much about our dear uncle. *Don't* worry about catching acute ratitis. *Don't* think about the fact that this was his ROOM. And *don't* think about the fact that he DIED right here in this bed. *Don't* think about the fact that we will bury him tomorrow, and *don't* think about the legend of Penny Pincher Castle — you know, the one about it being full of ghosts. I guess what I mean is . . . sweet dreams!"

BEFORE HE LEFT, HE BLEW HIS SNOUT ON THE COLLAR OF MY JACKET.

"Uncle, don't you have a tissue?" I groaned.

He nodded mournfully. "I do have one, but

I don't want to use it up!"

Once he was gone, I slipped under the covers fully clothed. I was **freezing** my tail off!

I tried to think happy thoughts. But it was hard. *"Oh, for the love of all that's warm and cheesy . . .* what mouse bumps!"

I had the mouse bumps because:

a) I was in the dark! Uncle Samuel took the candle with him (to save money!).

b) It was terribly cold! The flames in the fireplace weren't real, but were painted on (to save money!).

c) I kept hearing creepy noises! The windows creaked. The glass was broken and hadn't been repaired (to save money!).

d) I was petrified! It was so drafty the curtains blew around and looked like ghosts!

NIGHT FRIGHTS!

I tried to sleep, but I couldn't. I was TOO AFRAID!

It was a dark and stormy night. LIGHTNING BOLTS lit up the windows and cast SPOOKY shadows over the room. The wind whistled and seemed to whisper: BIGWIG...

BIGWIIIIIG...

BIIIIIIGWIIIIIIG...

I decided to go down to the kitchen to make myself some hot tea. Maybe I wouldn't be so terrified if I had a nice, full belly.

I tiptoed down the CREAKY staircase,

feeling my way carefully, because I didn't have a candle. I was almost glad of the darkness . . . who knows what horrors would have been visible if it had been light?

At last, I arrived in the kitchen. Thank goodness!

Just then, I heard someone pawing around behind the corner — and a **monstrous** shadow appeared on the wall! A huge, threatening paw was reaching for me! It looked like the claw of an enormouse cat!

"Wh-who's there?" I cried.

What could it be?

From behind the corner, out popped — THEA, **Trap**, and Benjamin!

"Huh? You're here, too?" they YELPED.

"Huh? You're here, too?" I YELPED.

"We wanted to make some hot **tea**," my sister explained.

It turned out making hot **tea** was easier said than done! We looked through all the cupboards and found only *one* tea bag, which, naturally, had been used!

While we **HEATED** up the water, I decided to confide in my family. "There's something **bizarre** about that coffin. It is way too light. It's very **strange**!"

"Hmm, well, why don't we go **check it out**?" Thea suggested. That's my sister for you. She's totally fearless!

I **shuddered** at the thought. The idea of touching that *thing* made my fur stand **on end**.

But not Thea's. She **scurried** into the room with the **coffin**. She felt around in the dark until she found it. Then she lifted the cover and cried out, **"IT'S EMPTYYYYYYYYY!"**

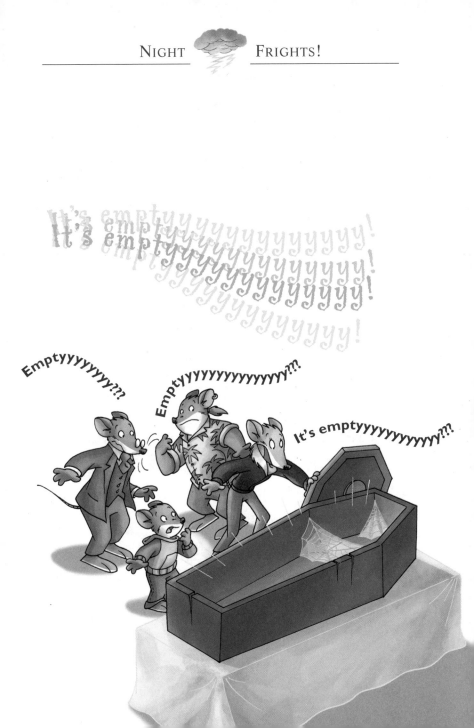

Stop, You Little Fur Ball!

"THE COFFIN IS EMPTY!"

Thea squeaked in disbelief.

"Wh-wh-what?" I stammered. "The coffin is empty?" I gulped. "Does that mean Uncle Bigwig has come back to **LIFE**?! Maybe — maybe he's a zombie!"

"Creepy cheese curls, where is Uncle Bigwig?" Trap screeched.

"What if Uncle Bigwig never existed?!" Benjamin whispered.

At that moment, I glimpsed a shadow slipping by us. By this time, my nerves were totally shattered. "Aaaaaaaaaaaaagh!!!" I shrieked.

The **shadow** was as quick as lightning. Faster than the mouse who ran up the clock, it **SPED** toward the corridor.

But Trap grabbed it by the tail. "Stop, you little fur ball!"

We lit a candle, which **REVEALED** a snout with hazel-colored **fur** and bushy white eyebrows.

"**WHAAAAAAT?**" we all shouted in shock.

"Huh?"

"Uncle Samuel?"

"What are you doing here?"

"And why is the coffin empty?"

"Oh, forgive me, my dears! I think I have a little explaining to do. . ."

IT WAS ALL A TRICK!

"Forgive you?!? Why?" Thea demanded.

"Just what do you need to explain?" Trap asked, looking skeptical.

By this time, we had made quite a ruckus. One by one, our other family members began trickling into the room. After a few minutes, all the *Stiltons* and all the **Stingysnouts** had arrived.

We listened in silence while Samuel tearfully tried to explain. "Okay, I will tell you everything — **absolutely everything**!" He took a deep breath before continuing. "A few weeks ago, I found an ancient scroll in one of the drawers in the **GReat Hall**. When I found this *scroll*, I was afraid that I

would have to share the castle with all of the **Stingysnouts** and all of the *Stiltons*," Uncle Samuel sobbed. "I am old, and I have lived my whole life in this **castle**. This is my home, and I am very attached to these walls! **I was afraid of losing my home. Do you understand?** I was so afraid I made up Uncle Bigwig and said he was the **SOLE** heir to the Stingysnout fortune. But Uncle Bigwig never existed! I pretended he left everything to me — I pretended he was **DEAD** . . . and I invited you all here for this *fake* ceremony to read his *fake* will, in which I *made believe* that he left me the **castle**."

Everyone stared at him in disbelief. Finally, Grandfather William found his squeak. "You mean, it was all *fake*?!"

"Yesssssss! It was all faaaaake!" Uncle Samuel screeched. "No one has died!

As of today, on the occasion of the marriage of Cheddar Cheapskate Stingysnout and Serena Stilton, the Stingysnout and Stilton families are bound together. From this day forward, they promise their eternal friendship.

With this scroll, Cheddar and Serena declare that just as their love will last for eternity, so too will these families forever be friends. They will share the castle in which their love did flourish.

And so Cheddar and Serena leave this castle to all the descendants of the Stingysnout and Stilton families, so that they may always live together in harmony, just as we two do.

In good faith,
Cheddar and Serena

Can you ever forgive me, my dear relatives?"

Thea shook her snout. "You found out the castle belonged to **ALL OF US**, and you wanted to keep it **aLL foR youRseLf**? That's terrible, Uncle Samuel."

No one knew what to do next. So all the *Stiltons* and all the **Stingysnouts** except me and Uncle Samuel shut themselves into the banquet hall to figure it out.

I stayed with **Uncle Samuel** to keep him company. He had been incredibly selfish, it's true, but I didn't want to leave him **alone**.

Uncle Samuel didn't say a word. He just wept quietly.

Finally the door burst open, and the family filed back into the room.

Trap **ANNOUNCED**, "The family has decided to forgive you, but . . ."

"**Hooray!** Thank you, thank you!"

Uncle Samuel rejoiced.

". . . but we have a few conditions," Trap continued. "First, you need to **reſtore** the castle. Next, you must invite **ALL** of us to spend our vacations here!" Trap paused. "And finally, you will pay for our room and board."

There was a moment's silence. Then Uncle Samuel muttered, "Restore the castle? Invite guests? Pay for your vacations?" His fur had turned paler than a slice of Swiss. "I see. So — *you want to bankrupt me!*"

With that, he ***fainted***.

Gulp!

HOW ABOUT A FEW JOKES?

Benjamin and I helped Uncle Samuel up when he **came to**. There was a moment of silence. Then Uncle Gagrat Stilton shouted, "Why so down in the snout, everyone? Never fear, Uncle Gagrat is here to lift your spirits! How about a few jokes?"

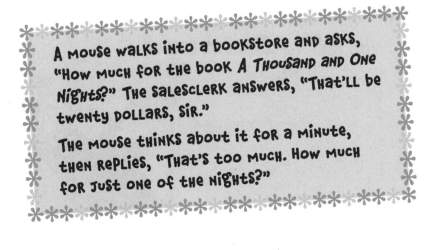

A mouse walks into a bookstore and asks, "How much for the book *A Thousand and One Nights?*" The salesclerk answers, "That'll be twenty dollars, sir."

The mouse thinks about it for a minute, then replies, "That's too much. How much for just one of the nights?"

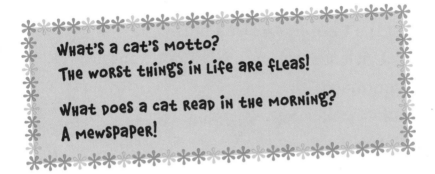

What's a cat's motto?
The worst things in life are fleas!

What does a cat read in the morning?
A mewspaper!

All of the *Stiltons* laughed — but none of the **Stingysnouts** did!

Uncle Gagrat giggled. "Okay, here's another one for you. . . ."

Why do lazy rats bake bread?
Because they want to loaf!

All of the *Stiltons* laughed — but none of the **Stingysnouts** did!

Uncle Gagrat pretended not to notice. He continued:

What does a ghost say when he makes a mistake?
"I made a boo-boo!"

How does a mouse feel after taking a shower?
Squeaky clean!

Once again, all of the *Stiltons* laughed — but none of the **Stingysnouts** did!

Uncle Gagrat rolled his eyes. "Oh, you didn't find that funny? I guess you mice didn't inherit the Stilton funny bone! Don't worry; I will explain everything later. . . ."

The Stingysnouts looked at him in confusion. They were whispering behind their **paws**, like they were trying to figure out why Uncle Gagrat was laughing so hard. It was obvious they didn't find his jokes funny. And that seemed to make them sad.

The **SADDEST** one of all was Chintzina, Uncle Samuel's younger sister. Chintzina never laughs — Uncle Samuel forbids it. He says that **laughing is a waste of energy**!

I looked at Chintzina more closely. It was hard to tell how old she was. She was dressed in drab, patched clothing. She still had curlers in her fur. When I thought about it, I realized she'd been wearing curlers every time I'd seen her! Who knew how she would have looked without them? It was as if they had become a permanent part of her head.

Chintzina knits in her spare time. Her specialty is **MULTICOLORED** socks, which she makes out of wool she finds here and there. "Put a sock in it, Chintzina! After all, that's the only thing you know how to make! Ha ha ha!" Uncle Samuel always teases her.

BUT WHO . . . BUT WHY?!

"I don't get it!" Uncle Gagrat shouted in frustration. "Don't you mice ever laugh? What about if someone tickles your paws with a feather? Not even then, I'll bet!"

He consulted his favorite book, *The Wacky Rat's Joklepedia*, and muttered, "Hrm, I think there's a *joke* in here somewhere about — ahh — yes — here it is!" He turned to the group and announced, "I'd like to dedicate this joke to a very special rodent, our dear Chintzina!"

SPECIAL!   SPECIAL!   SPECIAL!

WHAT IS COUSIN TRAP'S FAVORITE FOOD?
PRANK-FURTERS!

All of the *Stiltons* laughed — but none of the **Stingysnouts** did!

Until Aunt Chintzina

shut her eyes,

wrinkled her lips,

curled her whiskers,

and opened her mouth.

I thought she was about to sneeze, but instead . . .

SHE BURST OUT LAUGHING!

It was an extraordinary, **UPROARIOUS**, fabumouse laugh!

In fact, her laughter was so contagious

that all the other **Stingysnouts** began to laugh, too!

LAUGHTER IS CONTAGIOUS!

At that moment, Uncle Gagrat whispered, "Nephew, I think I'm in *love*. . . ."

"What? When did this happen?" I asked him.

"Just now!" he exclaimed.

I looked around. "But with whom?" I asked.

"With that *enchanting creature*!" he replied.

I looked around again. "What enchanting creature?" I asked in confusion.

He pointed one paw at Chintzina. "She is the rodent of my dreams!"

I was shocked. "But why?"

He sighed dreamily,

" *Aaaaaahhhh, I love her laugh. . . .* "

ONE WEEK LATER . . .

For the whole next week, Uncle Gagrat *courted* Aunt Chintzina with a vengeance. He was determined to win her over.

First he brought her a box of *heart*-shaped chocolates, but Uncle Samuel just shouted, "Eating these *sweets* will rot your teeth and cost money at the dentist!"

Poor Chintzina.

Next Uncle Gagrat tried to serenade her from beneath her window, but Uncle Samuel just shouted, "Save your squeak, you silly rodent!

you're wasting your breath and your time! And time is money!"

Poor Chintzina.

Next Uncle Gagrat got her a big bouquet of *flowers*, but Uncle Samuel just shouted, "Hmph! Why don't you buy her some vegetable seeds instead! At least then we could plant the seeds and eat the **VEGETABLES** to save money!"

Poor Chintzina.

Meanwhile, however, her love for Uncle Gagrat was growing.

At the end of the week, much to everyone's surprise, Aunt Chintzina and Uncle Gagrat **ANNOUNCED**, "We have some great news! We want to get married! In fact, we ARE getting married . . . in a week!"

AN ARTICHOKE BOUQUET

All of the *Stiltons* and all of the **Stingysnouts** were in shock!

"You really want to get married?"

Thea asked excitedly.

"In a week?"

asked Benjamin, his eyes wide.

"WHAAAAT? How much is that going to cost me?" Uncle Samuel shrieked. *"Are you trying to bankrupt me??"* Then he **FAINTED**.

I woke him up. "Uncle Samuel, it doesn't matter how much it costs! Look at Aunt Chintzina! She's happy!"

"Ohh, it's soooo romantic!" Thea sighed. "They're just like Romeo and Juliet!"

"First the **VACATIONS** at **My exPeNSe**, now a *wedding*," Uncle Samuel complained. "My family really **DOES** want to bankrupt me!"

He pulled out a tattered notebook and began to write down all sorts of **NUMBERS**. "Let's do the math. Dear Chintzina, no *wedding dress*: You

ROMEO AND JULIET is a famous tragedy written by the English poet and playwright William Shakespeare (1564-1616). It tells the story of two young lovers whose families, the Montagues and the Capulets, keep them apart because of a long-standing rivalry.

Wedding dress...

Wedding rings...

Refreshments...

Decorations...

Bouquet...

Invitations...

can get married in what you are wearing right now — a **BATHROBE** and curlers (to save money!). Instead of flowers in your bouquet, we can use a bunch of artichokes from the neighbors' garden (to save money!). Instead of printing wedding invitations, we can write them out by paw on a roll of toilet paper (to save money!). As for decorations, we won't have any centerpieces — instead, let's pick bunches of weeds from outside the moat (to save money!). And for the wedding rings, I have just the thing! Two plastic gold rings that I found in an Easter egg. I've been saving them for years, because I knew they'd be useful one day. We won't have a real *wedding reception*; we can eat in the kitchen (to save money!). It'll be **JUST** the three of us: you, your husband, and me (to save money!). And here's the

Wedding Menu:

Appetizer: 1 bean!

First course: 1 piece of spaghetti with 1 drop of tomato sauce and 1 basil leaf!

Second course: 1 shrimp!
Side dish: 1 leaf of lettuce, dressed with 1 drop of oil, 1 drop of vinegar, and 1 grain of salt!

Dessert: 1 crumb of cake and 1 chocolate!

Followed by: 1 drop of coffee!

Drinks: Unlimited water (from the faucet)!

menu I've drawn up (to save money!). . . ."

But **Chintzina** was sick of being bossed around by her cheapskate brother. She put her paw down.

"This is going to be the happiest day of my life!" she declared. "I want a real *wedding reception*! I want to share my joy with all of the rodents I hold dear. I'm going to invite *all of the Stiltons* and *all of the Stingysnouts* so I can share everything I have. *Loving* means sharing what you have, however **LARGE** or small it may be!"

Uncle Samuel buried his snout in his paws. "First the vacations at my expense, then the *wedding*, and now the *reception! You all really, really, really do want to bankrupt me!"

He *FAINTED* again.

Gulp!

MY, HOW YOU'VE CHANGED!

When we woke up the next day, Chintzina was nowhere to be found.

"Where is my sisteeeeerrrrrrr???" Uncle Samuel shrieked.

Trap giggled. "She went to New Mouse City. She said she needed to buy things for the wedding . . . **lots** of things!"

Uncle Samuel turned WHITER than fresh

mozzarella. Instinctively, his paw reached for his wallet. "B-b-buy things? F-f-for the wedding? L-l-lots of things?"

Trap nodded, smirking. "Uh-huh. And Chintzina didn't go alone. She was with her friends: *all of the Stiltons* and *all of the Stingysnouts*! She said she had to go to the FURDRESSER . . . to the *beautician* . . . to the tailOR . . . to the *florist* . . . to the perfume shop . . . to the **jewelry store** . . . and also to —"

Uncle Samuel cut him off with a shriek. "Noooooooooo! How much is all that going to cost me? *You meddling mice are really trying to bankrupt me!*"

He paced nervously for hours, waiting for Chintzina to return. When she finally scampered through the door, he ran to meet her. "Chintzina!" he gasped. "You've changed more than Lady RatRat at the MouseTV Music Awards!"

chintzina goes to the city

First Chintzina went to the beautician for a nice cheese face mask.

Now her fur is as soft as a peach!

Then she got contact lenses and went to the furdresser for a furcut.

Now she has a chic new do!

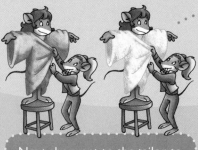

Next she went to the tailor to buy a wedding dress.

Now she doesn't have to wear patched clothing!

After that, Chintzina went to the flower shop to pick a bouquet for the wedding.

Now she's blooming like her flowers!

Then she went to the jewelry store and bought a new necklace.

Now she feels like a real glamour mouse!

Finally, she went to the perfume shop to get a new scent!

Now she smells as good as she looks!

LOVE IS THE BEST BEAUTY SECRET!

The rodent in front of us was unrecognizable.

It was Chintzina . . .

but it wasn't . . .

but it was!

"Yes, I've changed, Samuel," she said, smiling. "This morning I got up and said to myself, 'Enough with these curlers!' So I made a few **changes**. What do you think?"

Samuel opened his snout to ask, "What did all this cost?" But before he could, Uncle Gagrat threw himself adoringly at her paws. "Dear Chintzina, I thought you were beautiful before, but now you are really **stunning**!"

"It's true, you look *gorgeous*!" said Thea

approvingly. "That new furdo really brings out the **sparkle** in your eyes!"

Chintzina gave Uncle Gagrat a kiss on the whiskers. "Dearest Gagrat, it's not the **clothes**, the **jewelry**, and the perfume that make me look so beautiful! Your faith in me has helped me regain faith in myself! You've helped me REALIZE that the best beauty secret in the world is love!"

"Huh?" Uncle Samuel snorted. "love? A beauty secret?"

"Oh, yes," Chintzina sighed. "love changes you inside and out — and the best part is, it's *free*!"

Uncle Samuel stammered, "Y-yes, but the clothes, jewelry, and all the rest aren't *free*, and who will **PAY** for it? Chintzina doesn't have a dime!"

I was outraged at Uncle Samuel's shoddy treatment of his sister. So I stepped forward and said, "I will pay for it! Consider it my *wedding gift* to Aunt Chintzina."

Uncle Gagrat shook his snout. "That's very kind of you, Nephew, but I will pay. I am *happy* to make my future **wife** happy."

But Chintzina put out her paws to both

of us. "Thank you, Geronimo. Thank you, Gagrat. You are true *gentlemice*. But I don't need your help — I can pay for it on my own!"

"That's right!" Thea **SHOUTED**. "She can pay for it on her own!"

Uncle Samuel opened his eyes wide. "Huh? On her own? How?"

Aunt Chintzina giggled under her whiskers. "This morning, when I went out with my *friends*, I visited all of the boutiques in the city. And guess what, Samuel? I only know

how to make **socks**, but a lot of rodents like my socks! They are really *fashionable* in New Mouse City right now!"

Thea turned on the television. A journalist appeared and **announced**, "A new trend has spread through the city: **MULTICOLORED** socks! All the trendiest rodents simply MUST have a pair! The trend began this morning at the most fashionable boutique in the city. It seems that the socks are the work of a certain Chintzina *Stingysnout*. We are searching for her so she can give us an interview!"

A moment later, the phone rang: It was *journalists* looking for Chintzina! Every **boutique** on Mouse Island wanted to buy her socks. And the **bank** wanted to offer her a loan to open her own sock boutique!

"Way to go, Chintzina! Sock it to 'em!" cried Trap, giving her a hearty slap on the back.

We would like to give Chintzina Stingysnout a loan!

We would like to interview Chintzina Stingysnout!

We would like to order a hundred pairs of Chintzina Stingysnout's designer socks!

Love is good for you...

Love is good for you! It warms your heart.

Yes, love gets you off to a great start!

You'll find yourself smiling if love you learn —

Happiness, joy, and contentment you'll earn.

Love yourself above all.

Rich or poor's not important at all.

Inside your heart, you'll find life's true measure —

You'll discover love is your greatest treasure!

If you love the world and those around you,

You'll find that friends surround you.

Give them your trust, respect
their feelings.

You'll see love can do all kinds of
healing!

Love the nature that surrounds you:

Flowers, fields, and oceans around you!

Even a small insect should be respected.

All's worth loving, nothing neglected!

Love is good for you! It warms your heart.

Yes, love gets you off to a great start!

You'll find yourself smiling if love you learn —

Happiness, joy, and contentment you'll earn.

Love is good for you —

HOW ABOUT A DANCE?

The day of the wedding was upon us in no time. The ceremony was beautiful, and the food at the reception was *whisker-licking-good*! My cousin Trap cooked for everyone. He might be a trickster, but he's also a *fabumouse* chef!

After the meal, the *music* began.

It was right at that moment that I smelled some sweet *rose* perfume. A high-pitched squeak screeched in my ear: "Hi, Geronimo! Nice ceremony, isn't it?!"

It was *Zelda Stingysnout*, Stevie's journalist cousin! Her furdo was combed into a fluffy pompadour and she had a *red rose* pinned in front of her ear. She was wearing a black dress with a heart-shaped pendant inscribed with her initials, **Z.S.** On her paws were STEEL high heels that looked like they'd crush your toes if she happened to step on them.

"You're right, Zelda," I replied. "Chintzina and Uncle Gagrat make a great couple!"

Zelda winked at me. "Don't you think *we* would make a great couple, Geronimo? How about a dance?"

Name: Zelda
Last name: Stingysnout
Who she is: A distant relative of Geronimo Stilton
Profession: Journalist. She writes the "Romantic Rodent" column for The Daily Rat, rival newspaper of The Rodent's Gazette.
Distinguishing characteristics: She always wears a red rose in her furdo.

Before I could reply, Zelda grabbed my paw and dragged me out to the middle of the dance floor.

"Make spaaaace!" she shrieked to the rodents around us. Then she pulled me into a **sweeping** waltz, making me spin around like a top!

MARTIAL ARTS?!?

Desperate to make conversation as we **DANCED**, I asked *Zelda*, "So, you're an expert on **romance**, right? What do you do during your free time? Do you write poetry? Paint? Embroider?" Those were the most romantic hobbies I could think of.

"Of course not!" Zelda exclaimed. "Those are way too tame for a sportsmouse like me! I am a practitioner of **MARTIAL ARTS**."

"**MARTIAL ARTS?**" I asked, surprised. "Really?"

Ouch!

Oww!

"You betcha!" Zelda responded. "Here, let me show you. . . . ~ haaaiiiiiyaaaaaaaaaa!"

Before I could protest, Zelda began demonstrating her karate moves.

First she stuck a finger in my **EYE**.

Then she flung her paws against my **CHEST**.

Next she boxed my **ears** with the purse.

I fell **flat on my snout** in the middle of the room.

She twirled around. "Haaiiiyaaaa!!!" she shouted, stepping on my tail with her **STEEL** heels.

Haaiiiyaaaa!

Umphh!!

I lay on the floor, moaning like a gerbil who'd fallen off his wheel.

"Oh, dear!" Zelda cried. "For such a handsome mouse, you are awfully FRAGILE! But have no fear. Your Zelda-bear will take good care of you!"

When they saw me curled up on the floor, all the relatives gathered around and began gossiping.

"What happened?"

"Well, it looks like *Geronimo* wants to marry *Zelda*. He got down on his paws to propose!"

"Oh, that's so *romantic*!"

"So there's going to be another *wedding*!"

"Well, no, you see, she REJECTED him. . . ."

"Oh! I heard he's already dating someone. . . ."

"Yes, a certain Petunia Pretty Paws. . . ."

"What a fickle rodent he is!"

"Yes, Zelda is really mad. . . . She stepped on his tail with her **STEEL** heels. . . ."

"Poor Geronimo . . ."

At first, I was too weak to protest. But as soon as I got my breath back, I **yelled** with the last of my energy, *"Oh, for the love of cheese,* I don't want to get married! That is, er, I don't want to marry Zelda!"

Zelda put her paws on her hips. "Is that so, Geronimo? Well, that's good, because I wouldn't marry you if you were the **last** rodent on Mouse Island!" She turned her tail and stomped off, her steel heels clicking.

I sighed with **relief**. That Zelda was quite a mouse!

A LONG, LONG, LONG TRIP

I said good-bye to **Uncle Samuel** and all the other *Stingysnouts*, who hugged me one by one. By now we had become good friends! I even said good-bye to *Zelda*, who had decided to forgive me. She whispered in my ear, "So, handsome, when will see each other again?"

Kiss, kiss!

BLUSHING, I replied, "Good-bye, Zelda. Er, I'm sure we'll see each other again — sooner or later!"

I jumped in Thea's car to **LEAVE** for New Mouse City.

"Come on, Thea. We're leaving!" I shouted.

As soon as we drove out of sight, I let out a sigh of relief. Zelda meant **well**, but I am way too big a 'fraidy mouse to date her!

We drove all **NIGHT**, until finally, at dawn, we reached New Mouse City.

I stopped at home to drop off my bags. I took a quick shower, nibbled on a **snack** (hot cheese and a cheddar muffin), and then scampered over to *The Rodent's Gazette*.

I entered the office **WHISTLING**. I am always in a good mood when I go to work, because I love my job! Plus all the rodents who work at the newspaper are my friends.

I scurried into the editorial office. The reporters, photographers, illustrators, and designers were all busy in a meeting.

Who knew what they were squeaking about?

I'M A DEAD
MOOOOUUUUUSE!

"What are you squeaking about?"
I asked curiously.

"Geronimo, while you were away, we thought of a **new idea**," Priscilla Prettywhiskers answered.

I smiled. "Great! I love new ideas."

"You remember we were supposed to *create a new column*?" Priscilla continued.

"Oh, yes, of course, the new column!" I replied.

"Well, we realized we didn't have a *romance* column, so we approached the most famouse love expert in all of New Mouse City. She used to work for *The Daily Rat*, but I am happy to tell you, Geronimo, that this rodent (who coincidentally is an admirer of yours) *has already signed a contract*!"

A light went off in my head.

Romance column?

The most famouse love expert?

An admirer of mine?

"In fact, I believe she is also one of your distant relatives," Priscilla went on. "Her name is . . ."

Romance column?

The most famouse love expert?

An admirer of mine?

I leaped up. **"WHAT'S HER NAME???"**

Shorty Tao, Patty Plumprat, Gigi Gogo, Merenguita Gingermouse, and Dolly Fastpaws all shouted, "Her name is *Zelda Stingysnout*!!!"

"Zelda Stingysnout?" I gasped. "Holey cheese, I am a **DEAD MOUUUUUSE**!"

At that moment, I heard a familiar squeak. "**Hey, handSome**, aren't you thrilled? I'm coming to work for you! Now we can see each other every day! Are you happy now, *you* fine-furred fellow? Kissy kissy kissy, you adorable mouse, you lovable rat, you sweet little snuggle bunny!"

That was the last thing I heard before I **FAINTED**.

My staff had to revive me with **stinky cheese** salts.

Well, dear reader, I bet you'd like to know what happened once Zelda came to work with us. And I'd **like** to tell you. But that's a story for another day, or my name isn't *Geronimo Stilton*!

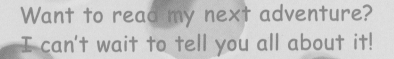

Want to read my next adventure?
I can't wait to tell you all about it!

RUN FOR THE
HILLS, GERONIMO!

I, Geronimo Stilton, was about to leave for a relaxing vacation all by myself. I was ready to kick back and connect with nature. But somehow, my peaceful trip turned into a crazy treasure hunt in the beautiful Black Hills of South Dakota—with the entire Stilton clan in tow! Our journey even included a hot-air balloon ride to Mount Rushmore. Holey cheese! What an adventure!

And don't miss any of my other fabumouse adventures!

#1 Lost Treasure of the Emerald Eye

#2 The Curse of the Cheese Pyramid

#3 Cat and Mouse in a Haunted House

#4 I'm Too Fond of My Fur!

#5 Four Mice Deep in the Jungle

#6 Paws Off, Cheddarface!

#7 Red Pizzas for a Blue Count

#8 Attack of the Bandit Cats

#9 A Fabumouse Vacation for Geronimo

#10 All Because of a Cup of Coffee

#11 It's Halloween, You 'Fraidy Mouse!

#12 Merry Christmas, Geronimo!

#13 The Phantom of the Subway

#14 The Temple of the Ruby of Fire

#15 The Mona Mousa Code

#16 A Cheese-Colored Camper

#17 Watch Your Whiskers, Stilton!

#18 Shipwreck on the Pirate Islands

#19 My Name Is Stilton, Geronimo Stilton

#20 Surf's Up, Geronimo!

#21 The Wild, Wild West

#22 The Secret of Cacklefur Castle

A Christmas Tale

#23 Valentine's Day Disaster

#24 Field Trip to Niagara Falls

#25 The Search for Sunken Treasure

#26 The Mummy with No Name

#27 The Christmas Toy Factory

#28 Wedding Crasher

#29 Down and Out Down Under

#30 The Mouse Island Marathon

#31 The Mysterious Cheese Thief

Christmas Catastrophe

#32 Valley of the Giant Skeletons

#33 Geronimo and the Gold Medal Mystery

#34 Geronimo Stilton, Secret Agent

#35 A Very Merry Christmas

#36 Geronimo's Valentine

#37 The Race Across America

#38 A Fabumouse School Adventure

#39 Singing Sensation

#40 The Karate Mouse

#41 Mighty Mount Kilimanjaro

#42 The Peculiar Pumpkin Thief

#43 I'm Not a Supermouse!

#44 The Giant Diamond Robbery

#45 Save the White Whale!

#46 The Haunted Castle

And coming soon!

#47 Run for the Hills, Geronimo!

Be sure to check out these exciting Thea Sisters adventures:

THEA STILTON
AND THE
DRAGON'S CODE

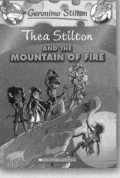

THEA STILTON
AND THE
MOUNTAIN OF FIRE

THEA STILTON
AND THE GHOST OF
THE SHIPWRECK

THEA STILTON
AND THE
SECRET CITY

THEA STILTON
AND THE MYSTERY
IN PARIS

THEA STILTON
AND THE CHERRY
BLOSSOM ADVENTURE

THEA STILTON
AND THE
STAR CASTAWAYS

THEA STILTON:
BIG TROUBLE IN
THE BIG APPLE

Meet
CREEPELLA VON CACKLEFUR

I, *Geronimo Stilton*, have a lot of mouse
friends, but none as **spooky** as my friend
CREEPELLA VON CACKLEFUR! She is an
enchanting and MYSTERIOUS mouse
with a pet bat named **Bitewing**.
YIKES! I'm a real 'fraidy mouse, but
even I think CREEPELLA and her family are
AWFULLY fascinating. I can't wait for
you to read all about CREEPELLA in these
fa-mouse-ly funny and **spectacularly
spooky** tales!

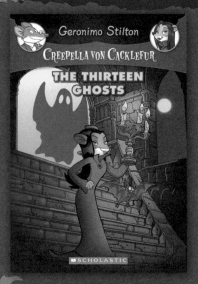

#1 THE THIRTEEN GHOSTS   **#2 MEET ME IN HORRORWOOD**

ABOUT THE AUTHOR

 Born in New Mouse City, Mouse Island, **GERONIMO STILTON** is Rattus Emeritus of Mousomorphic Literature and of Neo-Ratonic Comparative Philosophy. For the past twenty years, he has been running *The Rodent's Gazette,* New Mouse City's most widely read daily newspaper.

Stilton was awarded the Ratitzer Prize for his scoops on *The Curse of the Cheese Pyramid* and *The Search for Sunken Treasure.* He has also received the Andersen 2000 Prize for Personality of the Year. One of his bestsellers won the 2002 eBook Award for world's best ratlings' electronic book. His works have been published all over the globe.

In his spare time, Mr. Stilton collects antique cheese rinds and plays golf. But what he most enjoys is telling stories to his nephew Benjamin.

1. Main entrance
2. Printing presses (where the books and newspaper are printed)
3. Accounts department
4. Editorial room (where the editors, illustrators, and designers work)
5. Geronimo Stilton's office
6. Helicopter landing pad

THE RODENT'S GAZETTE

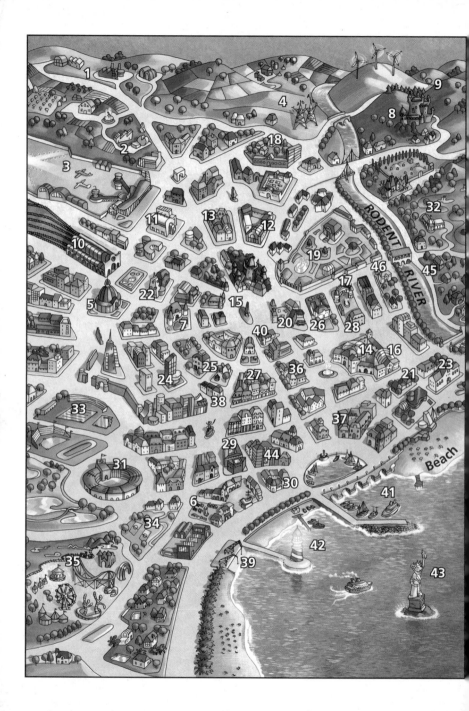

RODENT RIVER

Beach

Map of New Mouse City

Map of Mouse Island

1. Big Ice Lake
2. Frozen Fur Peak
3. Slipperyslopes Glacier
4. Coldcreeps Peak
5. Ratzikistan
6. Transratania
7. Mount Vamp
8. Roastedrat Volcano
9. Brimstone Lake
10. Poopedcat Pass
11. Stinko Peak
12. Dark Forest
13. Vain Vampires Valley
14. Goose Bumps Gorge
15. The Shadow Line Pass
16. Penny Pincher Castle
17. Nature Reserve Park
18. Las Ratayas Marinas
19. Fossil Forest
20. Lake Lake

21. Lake Lakelake
22. Lake Lakelakelake
23. Cheddar Crag
24. Cannycat Castle
25. Valley of the Giant Sequoia
26. Cheddar Springs
27. Sulfurous Swamp
28. Old Reliable Geyser
29. Vole Vale
30. Ravingrat Ravine
31. Gnat Marshes
32. Munster Highlands
33. Mousehara Desert
34. Oasis of the Sweaty Camel
35. Cabbagehead Hill
36. Rattytrap Jungle
37. Rio Mosquito

Dear mouse friends,
Thanks for reading, and farewell
till the next book.
It'll be another whisker-licking-good
adventure, and that's a promise!

Geronimo Stilton